David Walliams

PRESENTS...

THERE'S A SNAKE

Miss Bloat

The boring bits

First published in hardback by HarperCollins *Children's Books* in 2016

First published in paperback in 2017

HarperCollins *Children's Books* is a division of HarperCollins *Publishers* Ltd.

Text © David Walliams 2016. Illustrations © Tony Ross 2016

Cover lettering of author's name © Quentin Blake 2010

David Walliams and Tony Ross assert the moral right to be identified as the author and illustrator of the work.

A CIP catalogue record for this title is available from the British Library.

1 London Bridge Street, London SE1 9GF.

1 3 5 7 9 10 8 6 4 2

Printed and bound in China

ISBN: 978-0-00-817276-3

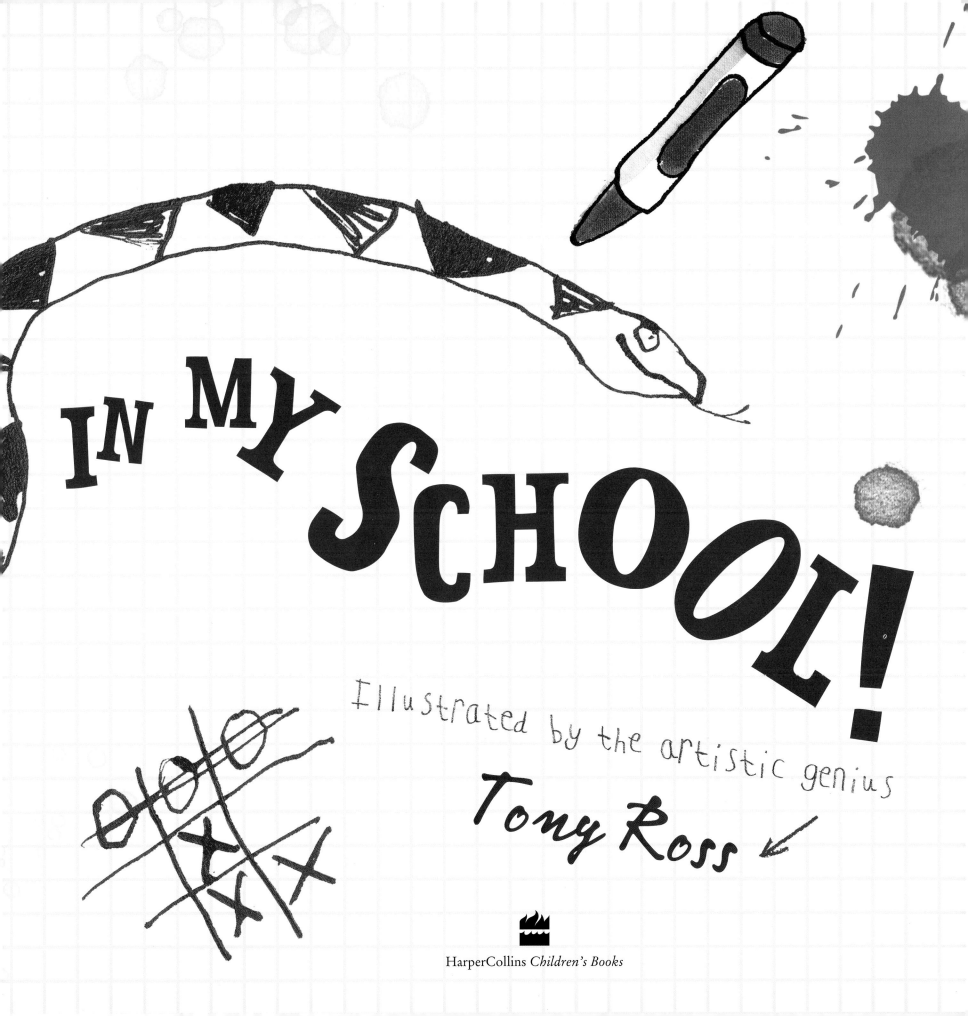

IN MY SCHOOL!

Illustrated by the artistic genius

Tony Ross

HarperCollins *Children's Books*

David
and
Bert

Stanley

Tony

Dorothy

To the Three Amigos,
Eddie, Frankie
and Alfred.
D.W.

To Ruth, with thanks.
T.R.

I ♥ CATS

Mr Bright had told all the children in his class it was Bring-your-pet-to-school Day. Everyone rushed into the playground to meet the animals. There was...

a *stupidly cute* gerbil,

a **tiny** goldfish,

a **FAT** cat,

a one-hundred-year-old tortoise

and a **tall** dog.

Last to arrive, as usual, was a little girl called Miranda.
She was riding on the back of an **enormous, slithery snake.**
"Meet Penelope, my pet python!"
announced Miranda.

On seeing the snake the other children screamed,

"Aaarrgh!"

Miranda **loved** being different. She always stood out at school with her

individual take on school uniform,   her cartwheels down the corridors

and her funny answers in class.

"What ended in 1945?"

"1944?"

Ha ha ha ha ha!

A python is a rather unusual pet but Miranda and Penelope had **so much fun** playing together. For the little girl the snake would pretend to be…

a balloon,

a scarf,

a hula-hoop,

a telescope,

a trombone…

and sometimes when they were both feeling particularly mischievous…

a third arm!

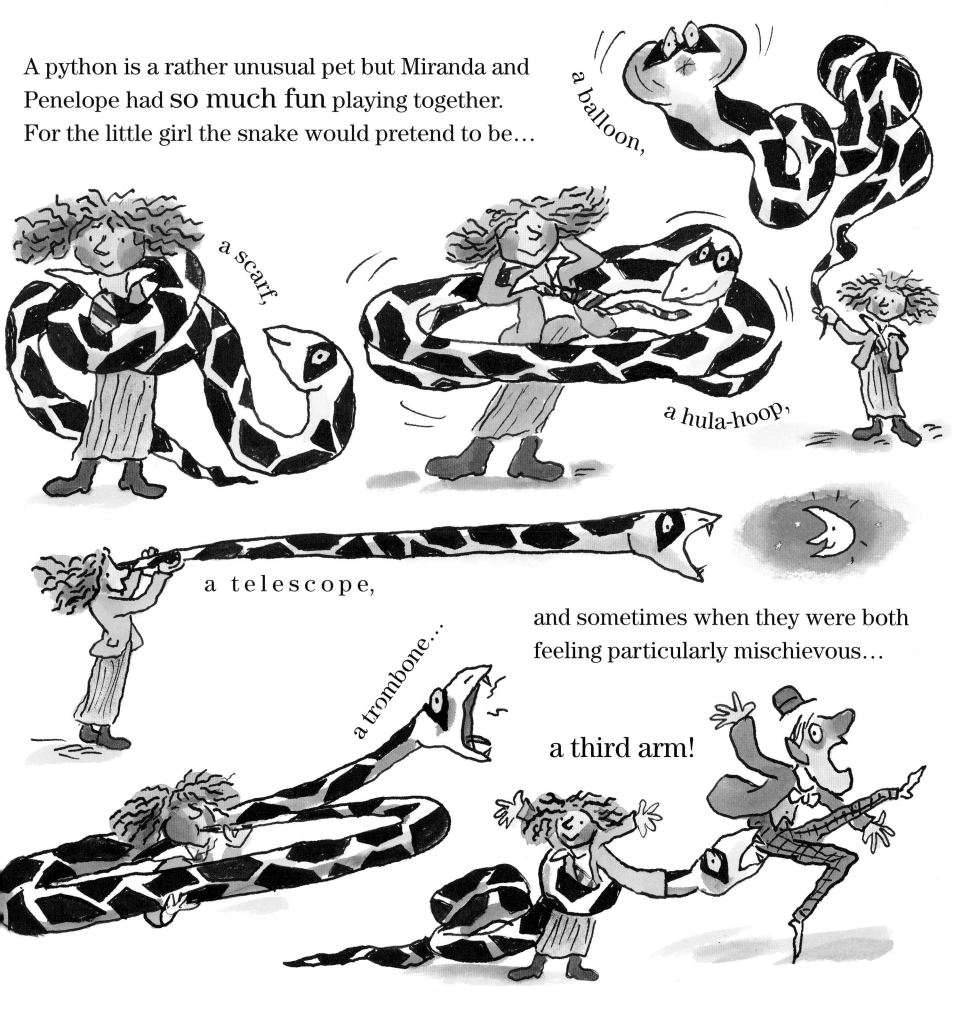

"Come and give her a **tickle**," encouraged Miranda.
But the other children were too scared.
Penelope was a python, after all.
And pythons **EAT** people.
All the pets were frightened too.

The **large** dog
yanked on his lead,
sending his tiny
owner flying.

The **goldfish**
tried to hide
behind **some
water**.

The **tortoise**
made a rather
slooooooooooow run
for it.

The cute **gerbil** flashed her gnashers and didn't look so cute any more.

The **FAT** cat just carried on napping.

Miranda slid down her snake.

The little girl **tickled** her python under the chin, and the snake smiled. "See? She's very friendly."

Soon everyone was gathered
around to marvel at Penelope.

The python loved the attention and made…

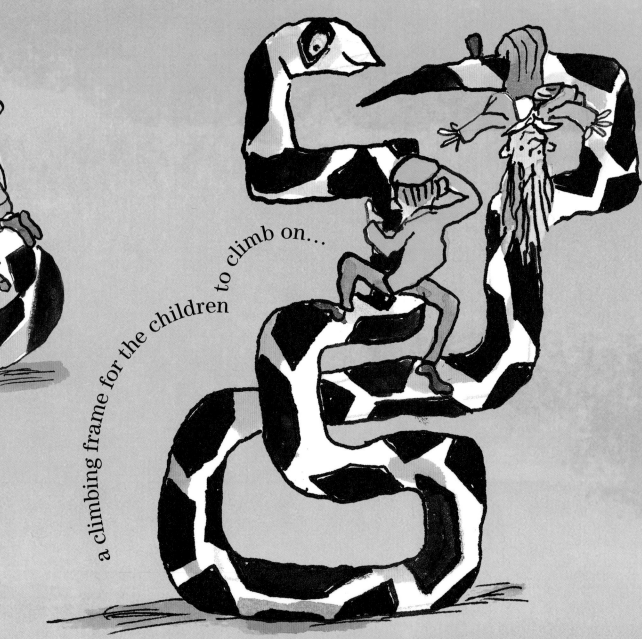

a climbing frame for the children to climb on…

steps for them to step up…

and a fireman's pole for them to slide back down.

Penelope even helped the children learn their numbers, although she could only go up to 9.

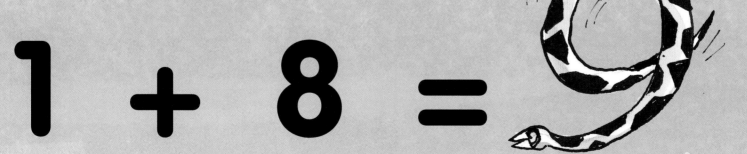

1 + 8 =

This was turning into the **best day of school ever.** But then…

Miss Bloat, the headmistress, thundered into the playground.

Miss Bloat didn't like animals much. Or children.

"It's Bring-your-pet-to-school Day," spluttered Mr Bright.

"And Penelope is my pet," said Miranda.

"Miranda! I should have known YOU would have to be different. A snake is not a PET! It's a MENACE!" snapped Miss Bloat.

"Mr Bright, all these filthy beasts are confiscated!"

All the girls and boys shouted,

"NOOOO!"

...as the headmistress stuffed their pets into the
LOST PROPERTY CUPBOARD!

Except for Penelope the snake.
Miss Bloat had other ideas for her...

"This disgusting thing is coming with me," bellowed the headmistress.
With that, she dragged the poor python along the corridor to her office.
"Where are you going to put Penelope?" asked Miranda.

"In the BIN!"

Miss Bloat crammed the snake into her bin and **slammed** the lid shut.
Then she plonked herself down on top so the python couldn't
escape. The bin rattled and rattled but...
Penelope was **trapped.**

Downstairs in the classroom, tears rolled down Miranda's cheeks. All the children were sad to have had their pets taken away, but no one was sadder than Miranda. The little girl feared she would never see Penelope again.

At the end of the day Miranda dashed upstairs to Miss Bloat's office to try to make her change her mind.

There was no answer, so slowly Miranda pushed open the door, only to see…

Penelope sitting in the headmistress's chair!

Miranda ran towards her pet and gave her a humongous hug.

Miss Bloat was nowhere to be seen, so the girl grabbed the key on the desk…

ran to the **LOST PROPERTY CUPBOARD** as fast as she could and unlocked it. The animals were overjoyed to be set free.

Z Z Z Z

WHOOOO

Then Miranda and all the pets slid down Penelope's back into the playground.

Penelope entertained everybody again.
She made…

a see-saw for them

to see-saw on…

a swing for them

to swing on…

a wheel for them to roll in…

and a skipping rope to skip with.

Penelope even helped some of the younger children with the alphabet, although it was hard to do an "X".

U V W X Y Z

As for Miss Bloat, she had completely disappeared. So Mr Bright was made headmaster. Now the children were allowed to bring in all their favourite animals whenever they wanted. The school became home to every sort of fantastic creature…

a giraffe,

an ostrich,

a tiger,

a gorilla,

an elephant,

a kangaroo,

a crocodile,

a grizzly bear...

and even a colony of penguins.

But the **STAR ATTRACTION** was always Penelope.

Though Miranda had noticed that there was something different about her python…

There was a bulge.

A **BIG** bulge in the snake's tummy.

A bulge in the shape of Miss Bloat.

But the little girl thought it best not to say anything.